Nov. 28, 2011

Written by
James Gelsey

A
LITTLE APPLE
PAPERBACK

SCHOLASTIC INC.
New York Toronto London Auckland Sydney
Mexico City New Delhi Hong Kong

Cataloging-in-Publication Data

Gelsey, James.
   Scooby-Doo! and the zombie's treasure / written by James Gelsey
 -- Reinforced library bound ed.
      p. cm. -- (Scooby-Doo mysteries)
   Summary: Scooby and the gang are going camping, but no ghost stories will be told around this campfire! A treasure-stealing zombie is haunting the campsite.
1. Camping--Fiction. 2. Zombies--Fiction. 3. Mystery and detective stories.
4. Dogs--Fiction. 5. Scooby-Doo (Fictitious character)--Juvenile fiction.
   [Fic] --dc 21

   ISBN 978-1-59961-896-8 (reinforced library bound edition)

"**W**hooooaaaaaa!" Shaggy called from the back of the Mystery Machine. Fred steered the van around a big curve in the road.

THUD.

"What was that?" Daphne asked. "Are you two all right back there?" She was sitting in the front seat with Velma and Fred.

"Like, no problem," Shaggy replied. Shaggy tried to see around the pile of camping supplies that had fallen over in the back of the van. "Except that I can't find Scooby-Doo. I think he's lost under the pile of camping equipment.

"Scooby-Doo? Are you in there?" Shaggy

asked. Shaggy lifted one bag up and moved another aside. He peeked under one of the tents that had come unrolled. There was Scooby-Doo, eating from a large basket of food.

"Like, who needs the great outdoors when you have all this great food indoors, right, Scoob?" Shaggy asked. He sat down next to Scooby and started eating.

"Will you two please straighten things up back there?" Fred called. "We'll be at the

campsite soon."

"And it would be nice if we had some food left over for the rest of the camping trip," Velma added.

"Like, don't worry," Shaggy called. "Scooby and I are only eating the pizza."

"I don't remember packing any pizza," Daphne said.

"Scooby and I did," Shaggy replied. "You didn't expect us to eat the stuff you brought, did you?"

"Hold on, gang," Fred called. "The road's going to get a little bumpy." He turned off the highway and onto a dirt road. It had just rained, and there were lots of puddles.

"Are you sure this is the way?" Daphne asked.

"Absolutely," Velma answered. "According to this guidebook, Treasure Bend is just a few miles away. This road has been here for over one hundred years."

"Like, you'd think someone would've

paved it by now," Shaggy said.

"The road was built by the people who discovered the gold mine," Velma read. "That's where the campsite gets its name. The gold mine is right next door."

"I wonder if there's any gold still left in there," Daphne said.

"The mine has been shut down for years," Velma said. "The campsite is the only thing up here."

Just then a large black car raced past the Mystery Machine. The car splashed through a big puddle, throwing mud all over the van. The car continued on its way.

"Jinkies, that car sure is driving quickly,"

Velma said.

"And messily," Shaggy added. "Like, our windows are covered with mud."

Fred pulled off to the side of the dirt road and turned on the windshield wipers. Mud splattered off of the van.

A police car drove up next to the van. The driver rolled down his window.

"Excuse me, son," the officer said. "Everything all right?"

"Fine, Offi-cer," Fred replied. "Except for the mud on our van."

"What brings you up to these parts?" the policeman asked.

"Camping," Daphne answered through the van's window. "At Treasure Bend."

"Okay, but be careful," the officer said. "I'm Sheriff Flugel. We've gotten reports of a jewel thief heading up to this area. He's been committing robberies around the local towns for a few weeks now."

"Is the thief dangerous, Sheriff?" Velma asked.

"Could be," he replied, "though he hasn't

hurt anyone yet. I'd reconsider that camping trip if I were you."

"Thank you, Sheriff," Fred said. Sheriff Flugel rolled up his window and drove away.

"Like, what's the holdup?" Shaggy called from the back of the van. "Scooby and I are on our last slice of pizza."

"The sheriff sounded serious," Daphne said. "Do you think we should stay?"

"I think we have a better chance of getting Shaggy and Scooby to stop eating than meeting a jewel thief out here," Velma said.

"Velma's right," Fred said. "So let's get going."

Chapter 2

Fred steered the Mystery Machine into the Treasure Bend campground. He parked in front of the main lodge. Everyone got out of the van.

"Hey, that looks like the car that splashed us with mud," Daphne said. She pointed to a black car next to them.

The gang walked onto the lodge porch. There was a man talking to a woman. He was holding several long cardboard tubes under one of his arms. His glasses kept slipping down his nose.

"I wonder what that's all about," Velma said.

"Like, maybe he's selling three-foot-long hot dogs," Shaggy suggested.

Scooby's eyes lit up. "Yum!" he barked, licking his lips with his big pink tongue.

"I'll bet that woman is Dot," Fred said. "She owns the campsite."

"Look here, Mrs. Butler," the man said as he unrolled another big sheet of paper. "This map shows where your property overlaps the underground mine." As the man pointed to a spot on the paper, he dropped the cardboard tubes on the ground.

One of the tubes rolled toward Scooby-Doo. Scooby bent down, picked it up in his mouth, and brought it to the man.

"Thank you," he said.

"Can I help you kids?" the woman asked.

"We're looking for the owner," Fred responded.

"Well, you've found her," the woman said. "I'm Dot Butler. And you must be that group who's here for the weekend. Welcome to Treasure Bend."

"Thanks," Fred said. "I'm Fred. We spoke on the phone. This is Daphne, Velma, Shaggy, and Scooby-Doo."

"Pleased to meet you," Dot said. "This is Professor Mullins."

"From the university," he said.

"Professor Mullins was just telling me that I should close down the campsite," Dot explained.

"I believe you should close the site," Professor Mullins said. "According to these maps, tunnels from the gold mine run underneath the whole campsite. These tunnels aren't safe anymore and could collapse at any minute."

"Then these must be geologic maps of the area," Velma said.

"That's right, young lady," Professor Mullins said. "You and your friends should really consider leaving right now. You never know when one of these tunnels could collapse."

"Thanks for the warning," Fred said. "But we've been planning this trip for weeks. If Dot's staying open, we're staying put."

Everyone looked at Dot Butler, waiting for her decision.

"I've lived here for so many years," Dot said, "I may as well stay put for a little while longer.

11

I have made my decision. The campsite stays open."

Professor Mullins gathered up his maps. "I hope you'll reconsider, Mrs. Butler. I'd hate for someone to get stuck in the mine." He returned to his car and drove away quickly.

"Someone should teach him some manners," Dot said.

"Someone should teach him how to drive," Daphne added. "He nearly splashed the Mystery Machine again on his way out."

"I sure do appreciate you kids deciding to stay," Dot said. "Business hasn't been so good lately. I may have to close down the campsite."

"It will take more than a man with a bunch of maps to scare us away," Velma said.

Suddenly, a strange growling came from the woods behind the lodge.

"Zoinks!" Shaggy exclaimed. "Like, a

growling monster in the woods would keep
me away!" "Me, roo!" Scooby barked. They
jumped and ran toward the van.

Chapter 3

The growling sound grew louder. Scooby and Shaggy ducked behind a large pile of firewood stacked near the Mystery Machine. Shaggy poked his head up. "Like, the name of this campsite should be Monster Bend instead of Treasure Bend," he said.

"Reah, Ronster Rend," Scooby agreed.

Heavy footsteps walked across the porch. Shaggy and Scooby ducked down again. Something blocked the sunlight and cast a long shadow over them.

"Hey, who turned out the lights?" Shaggy asked. He and Scooby looked up and saw

14

a tall man with wild hair and a big grizzly beard.

"Rikes!" Scooby jumped up from behind the logs and into Daphne's arms.

"Hi, Jack," Dot said.

"Like, the monster has a name?" Shaggy asked.

"Shaggy!" Daphne scolded.

"It's all right," the man said. "It's my job to scare people."

"It is?" Velma asked.

"They call me Panther Jack," the man said.

"He lives in the woods and helps protect the animals," Dot explained. "He also helps me keep unwanted guests out of the campground."

"Like panthers?" Daphne asked.

"And messy campers," Jack added. "Except now something is even scaring the animals and the campers."

"Do you know what's doing it?" Fred asked.

"A strange creature with glow-in-the-dark eyes," Jack said.

"You've seen him?" Dot asked.

"Yes," Jack said. "But I haven't been able to catch him. He always manages to disappear whenever I get close. I'll get him, whatever he is. See you later, Dot." Jack walked off toward the woods.

"You know, between the creature and what Professor Mullins said," Dot added, "maybe you kids shouldn't stay here after all."

"I'm with Dot," Shaggy quickly said. "Let's take a vote. All those in favor of leaving, raise your hands."

Shaggy raised both his hands. Scooby-Doo coiled his tail into a spring and sat down on it. He raised all four paws into the air.

"The paws have it," Shaggy said. "Time to go. Scooby and I will wait in the van while you say your good-byes." Shaggy and Scooby started walking toward the van.

16

"Hold on, you two," Velma called. "We're not going anywhere."

"Like, we're not?" Shaggy said.

"No," Fred said.

"Dot, where should we pitch our tents?" Velma asked.

"Anywhere on that side of the campground," Dot replied. She pointed to a large area to the right of the lodge. "Not too many people are here, so you should have plenty of room."

"Is there a hose we can borrow to wash our Mystery Machine?" Daphne asked.

"Behind the lodge," Dot said. "Make yourselves at home."

"I'll drive the van around back," Fred said. "We'll get settled and then wash off the Mystery Machine."

"I've got a bad feeling about this place, Scoob," Shaggy said.

"Me roo," Scooby agreed.

Chapter 4

The gang all worked together to wash the Mystery Machine. Soon it was super clean.

"Hey, look who's back," Shaggy said. "It's the bad driver."

Everyone turned and saw the black car pull up next to the lodge.

"I wonder what he's doing back here," Velma said.

The car door opened, but instead of the professor an old woman stepped out. She wore black pants, a long-sleeved black shirt, and dark glasses. Wisps of white hair stuck out from under her wide-brimmed black hat.

"Hey, you!" she yelled at the gang. "Just what do you think you're doing here?"

"Like, washing our van," Shaggy replied.

"Well, I want you off my property this minute!" she yelled.

"Your property?" Velma said. "This campground belongs to Dot Butler."

"No, it belongs to me," the old woman said. "I've got the paper to prove it."

She took a small piece of paper from her pocket and slowly unfolded it. It was yellow with age and very brittle.

"Whose name do you see on this map?" she asked, holding out the paper.

Fred, Daphne, and Velma looked at it. "It says, 'Sam Kunkle,'" Fred said.

"That's right, and I'm Ida Kunkle," the woman stated. "Sam Kunkle was my great-grandfather."

"His name on an old map doesn't prove anything," Velma pointed out.

"Sure it does," Ida replied. "Sam Kunkle used to be a cook on a ranch around here. But one day he discovered this gold mine and claimed all the land around it. So I want you off my land and away from my treasure."

"Treasure? What treasure?" Shaggy asked.

"The treasure of Treasure Bend," Ida said. "But don't get any ideas. Jeb Wocket, my

21

great-grandfather's best friend, tried to steal the treasure. But he could never find it. He got lost in the mine tunnels and disappeared. Now he's a zombie who haunts the gold mine to this day, still looking for the treasure." She turned toward the lodge and started walking away. "You'd better leave soon or the zombie will come get you," she said.

"Rombie?" Scooby whimpered.

"That does it," Shaggy said. "We're going. This campground isn't big enough for the three of us."

"Three of you?" Daphne asked.

"Yeah. Me, Scooby, and the zombie," Shaggy replied. "Come on, Scoob." He and Scooby started walking away.

22

"Where are you two going?" Velma asked.

"As far away from the zombie as we can," Shaggy replied.

"While you're out there, why don't you gather some twigs and branches for our campfire?" Fred said.

"Forget it!" Shaggy called back. "Scooby-Doo and I don't do campfires."

"That's too bad," Velma said. "We're going to be making s'mores around the campfire."

Shaggy and Scooby stopped in their tracks.

"Did you say *s'mores*?" Shaggy asked.

"Yup," Daphne answered. "But since you two don't do campfires —"

"Twigs and branches, coming up," Shaggy said. "C'mon, Scooby-Doo. We've got some gathering to do."

Shaggy and Scooby walked off into the woods.

"Here's a path, Scooby," Shaggy said. "Let's see where it goes."

They followed a path and picked up some twigs along the way. Just ahead, a fallen tree blocked the path.

"Looks like Mother Nature is helping us out, Scooby," Shaggy said. "Here's all the wood we could possibly want for the campfire."

They started picking up twigs. Then they heard a moaning sound come from the woods.

"Ruh?" Scooby perked up his ears to listen. "Raggy?"

Shaggy listened for a moment, too. "Relax, Scoob," he said. "Like, it's just that creepy Panther Jack guy. He's probably trying to scare us. Just ignore him."

"Rokay," Scooby said with a shrug. They went back to gathering twigs. Scooby saw a really long twig on the ground. He tried to pick it up, but his paws were full. Just then, someone reached for the twig and picked it

24

up. Scooby looked up as the zombie reached over and dropped the twig into Scooby's paws. The zombie was seven feet tall and his eyes glowed red.

"Raggy!" Scooby barked. He let go of all his twigs, jumped on Shaggy's shoulders, and

wrapped his paws around Shaggy's face. Shaggy dropped his twigs.

"What's with you, Scooby-Doo?" Shaggy said. He pried Scooby's paws off his face.

Scooby pointed behind Shaggy with his tail. Shaggy slowly turned around and saw the zombie.

The zombie growled.

"Zoinks!" Shaggy exclaimed. "Zombie!"

Shaggy turned and ran through the woods.

"Relp!" Scooby barked, still perched on Shaggy's shoulders.

The zombie ran after them.

Chapter 5

The zombie chased Shaggy and Scooby through the woods.

"Run, Raggy!" Scooby barked. "Raster! Raster!"

"I can't run any faster with you on my shoulders, Scooby," Shaggy said. "So I'm making this your stop."

Shaggy stopped short and sent Scooby flying through the air. Scooby landed on all fours. The zombie moaned and growled as he got closer to Shaggy and Scooby. Shaggy leaped through the air and landed right on top of Scooby.

"Giddyap, Scooby!" Shaggy said. "Mr. Lightbulb Eyes is getting closer!"

Scooby started running with Shaggy riding on his back.

"Attaboy, Scoob," Shaggy said. "He'll never catch us now."

Shaggy turned to look behind him and saw the zombie reaching out and grabbing for Scooby's tail.

"Spoke too soon," Shaggy said. "Step on it, Scooby!"

Scooby ran a few more steps and jumped over a fallen log. He and Shaggy sailed through the air and crashed down on a big pile of leaves. They poked their heads up and looked around. The zombie was gone!

"Like, where'd he go?" Shaggy asked.

"Ri dunno," Scooby answered.

"Well, I'm not waiting to find out," Shaggy said. "Let's go find the others." He stood up and brushed the leaves off his shirt.

"Uh, do you know the way back to the campsite?" Shaggy asked.

"Uh-uh," Scooby replied.

"Great," Shaggy said. "First we get chased by the zombie, and now we're lost. What else can go wrong?"

"It could rain," a voice said.

"Very funny," Shaggy answered. "Hey, wait, who said that?"

Shaggy and Scooby looked at each other.

"Rikes!" Scooby barked. He and Shaggy dived back into the pile of leaves. They slowly raised their heads and looked around.

"Is it the zombie?" Shaggy asked.

"Since when does a zombie sound like me?" the voice said. Then Daphne stepped out from behind some bushes.

"Daphne!" Scooby barked. He ran over

and gave her a big hug and a huge, wet kiss.

"Like, Daphne," Shaggy said, "what are you doing out here?"

"I thought I'd go on a nature walk," Daphne replied. "There are lots of wonderful flowers and birds out here. What have you two been up to?"

"We saw the zombie!" Shaggy answered.

"You did?" Daphne asked with surprise. "A real zombie?"

"With light-up eyes and everything,"

Shaggy said. "Show her, Scoob."

Scooby stood up on his hind legs. He put his front paws straight out in front. He opened his eyes as wide as he could and started lurching along. He threw in a moan every step or two.

"And he almost got us, too," Shaggy added. "But then he suddenly disappeared."

"That's odd," Daphne said. "I wonder where he could've gone? Where did you see him last?"

"Over there, on the other side of that log," Shaggy said, pointing behind him. Daphne walked over to take a look.

"Be careful, Daphne," Shaggy warned.

"Of what?" Daphne asked. "There's nothing to be afraid of over heeeeeeeeeeere!"

Shaggy and Scooby heard a soft *thud*. They looked over. Daphne was gone.

"Daphne! Daphne!" Shaggy called. They ran over and saw a big hole in the ground. "Daphne? Are you down there?"

They didn't hear any answer.

"We have to find the others," Shaggy said. "They're not going to believe this. First we lose the zombie. Now we've lost Daphne! Come on, Scooby. And hurry!"

"**C**oming through!" Shaggy called. He and Scooby burst through the trees and ran straight through the campsite and into their tent. They knocked over the center pole and the tent collapsed around them. They tried to find their way out. The more they struggled, the more tangled they got.

Suddenly, Shaggy felt someone grab him from outside the tent.

"Help! Help!" Shaggy called. "The zombie's got us!"

"Just hold still," a familiar voice said. It was Panther Jack. "I'll help you get out."

A moment later, Panther Jack lifted the heavy tent off Shaggy and Scooby.

"Like, thanks, man," Shaggy said.

"What's going on?" Fred called. He ran over from the lodge with Velma and Dot.

"Like, the zombie's got Daphne!" Shaggy blurted out.

"Shaggy," Velma said, "there's no such thing as zombies."

"Then some other gruesome creature with night-light eyeballs got Daphne," Shaggy said. "Right, Scoob?"

"Reah." Scooby nodded. "Rike ris." Scooby stood up on his hind legs and did his zombie imitation again.

"Hey, Scoob, like, that's really good," Shaggy said.

"Rank rou," Scooby barked as he blushed.

"Will you two knock it off?" Fred said. "Where's Daphne?"

"Like, we've been trying to tell you," Shaggy said. "The zombie was chasing us and then he disappeared. We ran into Daphne, and the next thing we knew, she was gone, too."

"Do you think you could remember where it happened?" Fred asked.

"Oh, no, we're not going back into those woods," Shaggy said.

"Shaggy, we need to find Daphne," Velma said.

"Panther Jack will go with you," Dot offered. "He'll make sure nothing happens."

"Well . . ." Shaggy began.

"Great," Fred said. "Let's go. We don't have a moment to lose."

"Here we go again, Scoob," Shaggy moaned as they followed Fred, Velma, and Panther Jack back into the woods.

As they walked, something caught Scooby's attention. He started sniffing the ground. Fred, Velma, Panther Jack, and Shaggy followed Scooby through the woods.

"Are you sure this is the way?" Panther

Jack asked. He sounded a little irritated.

"Like, if there's one thing you can say about Scooby-Doo," Shaggy said, "it's that his nose always knows."

"But we've passed that same pine tree three times now," Panther Jack responded. "This is a waste of time. I'm going to look for this zombie by myself. Here, take this."

Panther Jack took a rope off from over his shoulder and handed it to Fred. Then he turned and ran off into the woods.

"Like, there goes our protection," Shaggy said. "I hope nothing happens to us now."

"Shaggy, are you and Scooby sure this is the way?" Velma asked.

Scooby started walking faster, his nose still to the ground.

"I'm telling you, Velma old pal," Shaggy said, running along. "He's on to something."

The four of them came upon a big fallen log.

"This is the place where the zombie disappeared," Shaggy said. "And right there is where Daphne disappeared."

"Great work, Scooby," Fred said. He and Velma walked over to the spot where Daphne

38

disappeared. They looked down and saw an opening in the ground.

"Daphne must have fallen through this hole," Fred said. "If we're going to find Daphne, someone has to go down there."

Shaggy and Scooby looked at each other and then at Fred.

"Like, you don't mean one of us, right?" Shaggy asked.

"Of course not," Fred said. "I need you two to hold on to the rope and lower me down. When I'm ready to come up, I'll give a single tug on the rope. Got it?"

"You betcha, Fred," Shaggy said. "You can count on us."

Fred wrapped one end of the rope around his waist. Then he took a flashlight out of his pocket. Shaggy grabbed on to the rope, and

Scooby grabbed on to Shaggy. They slowly lowered Fred down into the hole.

"Like, I hope he doesn't run into that zombie," Shaggy said. "Worse, I hope that zombie doesn't run into us."

Suddenly, they felt a hard tug on the rope.

"That's our cue, Scooby-Doo," Shaggy said. "Let's pull up Fred-eroo."

"Right," Scooby barked.

Shaggy and Scooby pulled on the rope and went flying over backward. They bumped into Velma, knocking her glasses off.

"Hey, watch it, you two," Velma said.

"Like, sorry, Velma," Shaggy said. Then he and Scooby looked down and saw that the rope had broken apart.

"Ruh-roh," Scooby barked.

"Velma, you'd better look at this," Shaggy said.

"I can't look at anything until I find my glasses," Velma said. "So how about you and Scooby help me find them?"

"But, Velma —" Shaggy began.

"No buts, Shaggy," Velma interrupted. "Please help me look."

Shaggy and Scooby looked around on the ground. Velma got down on her hands and knees and put her hand out to feel the ground.

"Hey, this ground is kind of bumpy,"

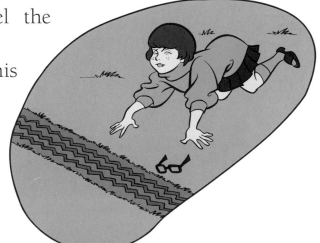

Velma said. "There's a strange pattern in the dirt over here."

Shaggy walked over to Velma.

"Here are your glasses, Velma," Shaggy said.

"Thanks," Velma said as she put her glasses back on.

Velma looked closely at the ground.

"Tire tracks!" she exclaimed. "It looks like someone drove a car through here just after it rained. Let's follow them."

They walked a few yards until the tracks stopped in front of an enormous bush. Velma walked up to the bush and gave it a shove. The bush rolled off to the side.

"Jinkies!" Velma exclaimed. "Look!"

A big black car was parked right in front of them.

"Judging by the location of this car," Velma said, "I'll bet that the gold mine entrance is right around here."

"You're right about that," a voice from the woods said.

"Ruh?" Scooby barked. He hid behind Shaggy for protection.

Fred and Daphne came out from behind a bush.

"Fred! Daphne! Boy, am I glad to see you!" Shaggy exclaimed.

Scooby jumped out from behind Shaggy. He gave Fred a great big hug. Then he gave Daphne a great big hug. Then he gave Fred another great big hug. Then he gave Daphne another great big hug.

"Okay, Scooby, thanks for the welcome," Daphne said.

"Like, what happened to you?" Shaggy asked.

"The hole Daphne and I fell into led to one of the abandoned tunnels in the gold mine," Fred said. "And look what we found inside."

Daphne took a piece of paper out of her pocket and unfolded it. It was an old map of the gold mine.

"And look what else," Daphne added. She showed the gang a pair of eyeglasses with small flashlights attached to them. The lightbulbs in the flashlights were bright red bulbs.

"Check out those groovy

glasses!" Shaggy said. "They are outta sight, right Scooby?"

"Roh reah," Scooby said.

"Hmm, I have a hunch that this zombie's haunting days are over," Velma said.

"I think you're right, Velma," Fred said. "Gang, it's time to set a trap."

Chapter 8

"Okay, here's the plan," Fred began. "That zombie will only come out if he believes that we're looking for the treasure."

"Like, what would make him think that?" Shaggy asked.

"I'm glad you asked, Shaggy," Fred said. "Because that's where you and Scooby come in."

Shaggy turned to Scooby. "Why do I always have to open my big mouth?" he asked.

"Ri dunno." Scooby shrugged.

"You two are going to pretend to be treasure hunters," Fred said, "and lure the zombie out. When he shows up, Scooby will keep him distracted. Shaggy and I will sneak up from behind and tie him up. Any questions?"

"Like, just one," Shaggy said. "Who's going to convince Scooby-Doo?"

Scooby was sitting on a big rock. He was looking up at the trees and whistling

"How about it, Scooby?" Fred asked. "Will you help us out?"

Scooby looked the other way and kept on whistling.

"Will you do it for a Scooby Snack?" Daphne asked.

Scooby stopped whistling for a moment. Then he started again.

"How about two Scooby Snacks?" Velma offered.

"Rokay!" Scooby barked. He leaped into the air as Velma and Daphne tossed the Scooby Snacks to him. Scooby gobbled them.

"Ranks!" Scooby barked.

"While you three take care of the zombie, I have a hunch I want to follow," Velma said. "And I'll need your help, Daphne."

"You got it," Daphne replied. She and Velma walked off into the woods.

"Shaggy and Scooby, you two start walking in that direction," Fred said. "Remember, you're looking for the treasure. I'll be right behind you in the woods."

Shaggy and Scooby walked slowly through the woods. They carried the map that Fred and Daphne had found in the mine.

"Like, according to this map," Shaggy said loudly, "we're close to the gold mine."

"Reah," Scooby barked loudly, nodding.

"That can only mean that the treasure is somewhere around here," Shaggy continued. "Right, Scooby? Right?"

Shaggy turned and saw Scooby standing in a small clearing. He was sniffing something on the ground.

"Like, what did you find, Scooby?" Shaggy called.

Scooby gave the object a small lick. "Mmmmmmmm," Scooby said. "Rocolate."

"Chocolate?" Shaggy said with surprise. He ran over to Scooby. "Hey, we must have dropped that when we were out here earlier. How about we share it, Scooby old pal?"

Just then, a loud moaning came from the woods behind them.

"Okay, Fred, you can have some, too," Shaggy called.

The moaning got louder. Shaggy and Scooby turned and saw the zombie lurching toward them.

"Zoinks!" Shaggy exclaimed. "The zombie! Quick, Scooby-Doo, get into position."

Shaggy quickly ran into the bushes to find Fred. Scooby opened up the map and pretended to read it. He heard the zombie getting closer.

"Raggy!" Scooby whimpered.

"Stay cool, Scoob," Shaggy whispered from the bushes. "We're almost ready."

The zombie was getting closer. Its eyes glowed fiercely. Scooby started backing away. He looked over the zombie's shoulder and saw Fred and Shaggy tiptoe out of the bushes. They reached up to throw the rope around the zombie.

Suddenly, the ground beneath Scooby gave way.

"Rikes!" Scooby barked as he tumbled into a hole. Scooby landed with a loud *thud* on a pile of dirt.

"Scooby!" Shaggy called.

Scooby shook the dirt off his head and looked around. He saw small lanterns hanging along the tunnel walls. Then he saw the

zombie fall through the roof of the tunnel to the ground.

"Rikes!" he barked again. Scooby jumped up and started running through the tunnel. The zombie stood up and chased after Scooby. Scooby spied a big metal bucket up ahead. He jumped into the air and dived in. When he landed, he felt the bucket shake. Then it started to move. Scooby poked his head up and looked around. He was in a runaway mine car!

Scooby turned and saw the zombie following in another mine car. The track went up and down, and the cars picked up speed.

Scooby saw the mine entrance just ahead. His mine car sailed off the track and out of the mine. Just before the car crashed, Scooby jumped out and landed in a flower patch.

The zombie's car flew out of the mine just behind Scooby's. The zombie's mine car crashed into a tree. The zombie went flying through the air and landed right on Scooby.

Chapter 9

F red and Shaggy ran over to the flower patch. They grabbed the zombie and tied him up. Dot showed up with Sheriff Flugel just as Velma, Daphne, and Panther Jack came out of the mine.

"Now we'll all see who this mysterious zombie really is," Velma said.

"Would you care to do the honors, Dot?" Fred asked.

"Yes, I would," Dot said. She reached over and yanked the mask off the zombie's head.

"Professor Mullins!" Dot exclaimed.

"Just as we thought," Velma said.

55

"But how did you kids know?" Sheriff Flugel asked.

"The only clue we had at first was that the zombie knew his way around this whole area," Velma said. "Especially the tunnels."

"Ida Kunkle and Panther Jack were suspects, too," Daphne continued, "because they also knew about the tunnels."

"All of them had reasons to keep people away," Fred said. "But then we found more clues."

"Like the eyeglasses with small flashlights on them," Velma said. "Perfect for making a zombie's glow-in-the-dark eyes."

"And perfect for someone who already wore glasses," Daphne added. "Like Professor Mullins and Ida Kunkle."

"Then there was the black car we found in the woods," Velma continued.

"And the map we found in the mine," Daphne said. "We knew we had seen one like it before."

She handed the map to Sheriff Flugel. He looked at it and then handed it to Dot.

"Why, it looks like one of the university's maps," Dot said. "The ones that Professor Mullins showed me."

"And the ones that the university reported stolen," Sheriff Flugel said.

"But that doesn't make sense," Dot said. "A professor wouldn't steal maps from his own university."

"But one of the most wanted men in the county would," Sheriff Flugel said. "This Professor Mullins is really Ronald Twitty, the jewel thief suspect I warned you about earlier."

"But why the zombie?" Dot asked.

"Because I had to make sure that no one would bother me here," Ronald Twitty said. "I heard about the story from that Ida Kunkle lady in town one day. The abandoned gold mine was a perfect hideout. And I would have gotten away with thousands of dollars in jewels, too. Except those kids and their pesky dog came and ruined everything."

"Tell it to the judge, Twitty," Sheriff Flugel said. He took Ronald Twitty by the shoulder and started walking.

"I'll give you a hand," Panther Jack said. "I'll meet you back at the campsite, Dot," he called over his shoulder.

"I can't thank you kids enough," Dot said. "Let's go back to the campground for a celebration."

When they got back, Scooby-Doo was already waiting for them. Panther Jack was just starting to build a huge campfire. Scooby sat by the fire holding a long stick in each paw and with his tail. At the end of each stick, marshmallows were slowly roasting in the campfire.

"Like, it looks like Scooby-Doo has found s'more treasure of his own," Shaggy laughed.

"Scooby-Dooby-Doo!" Scooby barked happily.

About the Author

As a boy, James Gelsey used to run home from school to watch the Scooby-Doo cartoons on television (only after finishing his homework). Today, he still enjoys watching them with his wife and two daughters. He also has a real dog named Scooby who loves nothing more than a good Scooby Snack!